Buddy's Bedtime

Happy Reading!

Pauleen O'Shea ☺

Buddy's Bedtime

Written by Pauleen O'Shea

Illustrated by Jason Dohanish

Idlehour Press

Published by Idlehour Press

For ordering information or special discounts for bulk purchases, please go to www.idlehourentertainment.com

Design and composition by Greenleaf Book Group LP

Library of Congress Control Number: 2006939178
ISBN 13: 978-0-9778063-0-0
ISBN 10: 0-9778063-0-8

Printed in China on acid-free paper

10 09 08 07   10 9 8 7 6 5 4 3 2 1

First Edition

For Buddy

Buddy loves to run and play, and chase his favorite ball.

But he stops and listens closely, when he hears his Mama call.

Mama made his favorite meal, chicken, carrots, and rice.

"And maybe if you're really good," she says, "You can have dessert tonight."

Buddy starts to gobble his food, and licks his bowl clean.

A yummy ice cream just for dogs is waiting especially for him.

Mama sees his bowl is empty, and reaches down to pick it up.

Buddy knows what's coming next, Mama's reaching in the cupboard.

To find his special ice cream
bowl, green in color
with white lettering.

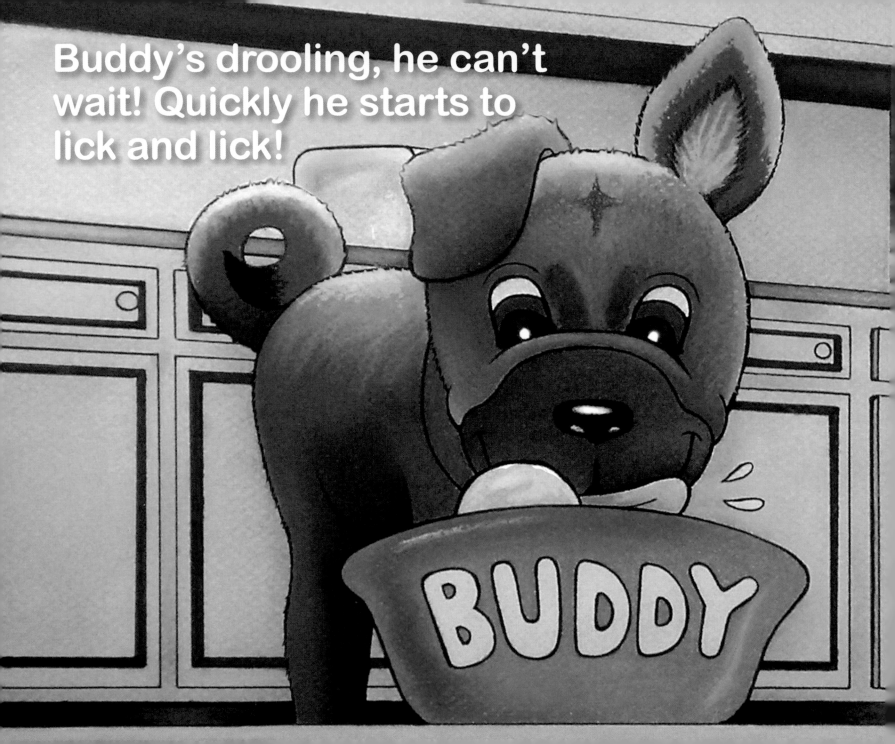

After that special treat, Buddy is feeling pretty happy.

But his full belly is making
him a little sleepy.

"Now Buddy," Mama says, "Before you get too tired, let's go outside and go potty."

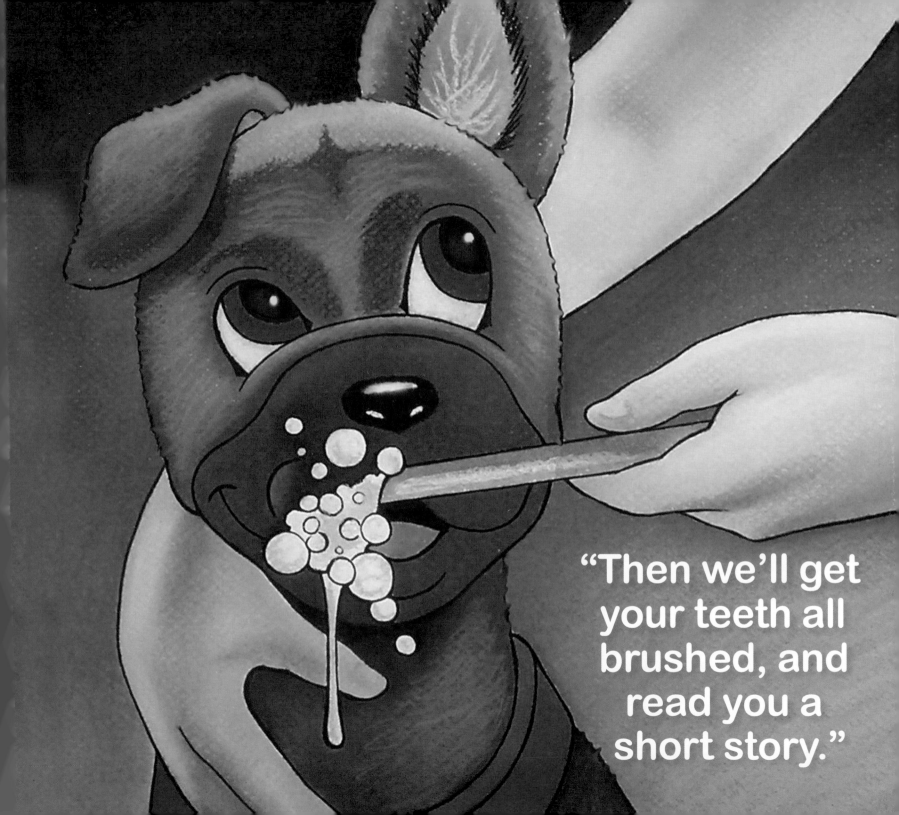

"Then we'll get your teeth all brushed, and read you a short story."

Buddy climbed onto his bed, as Mama began to read.

But as soon as his head hit the pillow, he began snoring.

So Mama
leaned down
and whispered
in his ear,

Showcasing stories that impart small life lessons to the reader, Buddy's First picture books for children help children correlate their own life experiences to those of Buddy—"The lovable, curly-tailed pup." Each book features a story that is easy to follow and emphasizes teaching values like the importance of good behavior, sharing, tolerance of others, problem solving, and safety.

For more information visit www.buddysfirst.com